S0-BIN-761

ana & andrew

Home Run

by Christine Platt
illustrated by Anuki López

Calico Kid

An Imprint of Magic Wagon
abdobooks.com

About the Author
Christine A. Platt is an author and scholar of African and African-American history. A beloved storyteller of the African diaspora, Christine enjoys writing historical fiction and non-fiction for people of all ages. You can learn more about her and her work at christineaplatt.com.

For every child, parent, caregiver and educator.
Thank you for reading Ana & Andrew! —CP

To the love of my life, for making me smile every single day. —AL

abdobooks.com

Published by Magic Wagon, a division of ABDO, PO Box 398166, Minneapolis, Minnesota 55439. Copyright © 2021 by Abdo Consulting Group, Inc. International copyrights reserved in all countries. No part of this book may be reproduced in any form without written permission from the publisher. Calico Kid™ is a trademark and logo of Magic Wagon.

Printed in the United States of America, North Mankato, Minnesota.
102020
012021

THIS BOOK CONTAINS
RECYCLED MATERIALS

Written by Christine Platt
Illustrated by Anuki López
Edited by Tyler Gieseke
Art Directed by Candice Keimig

Library of Congress Control Number: 2020941610

Publisher's Cataloging-in-Publication Data

Names: Platt, Christine, author. | López, Anuki, illustrator.
Title: Home run / by Christine Platt ; illustrated by Anuki López.
Description: Minneapolis, Minnesota : Magic Wagon, 2021. | Series: Ana & Andrew
Summary: Ana & Andrew are finally old enough to play team sports at the Recreation Center. Andrew tries out for the baseball team. They both learn about Jackie Robinson, the first African American to play in modern Major League Baseball.
Identifiers: ISBN 9781532139680 (lib. bdg.) | ISBN 9781644945223 (pbk.) | ISBN 9781532139963 (ebook) | ISBN 9781098230104 (Read-to-Me ebook)
Subjects: LCSH: African American families--Juvenile fiction. | Team sports--Juvenile fiction. | Baseball--Juvenile fiction. | Robinson, Jackie, 1919-1972--Juvenile fiction. | Professional sports—Juvenile fiction. | Sports--United States--History—Juvenile fiction.
Classification: DDC [E]--dc23

Table of Contents

Chapter #1
Choosing a Sport

Ana and Andrew loved sports. In the warmer months, they enjoyed swimming at the Recreation Center. When the weather was cool, they often went ice-skating with their family and friends.

But when Ana and Andrew swam, skated, or played other sports, they weren't members of a team. They were just having a good time.

So, of course, Ana and Andrew were excited once they were old enough to play sports at the Recreation Center. There were many different sports to choose from. They couldn't wait to play with teammates.

Ana tried out first. She loved playing basketball, so that was the sport she chose. Everyone was very excited when she made the team.

"Do you think the coach will let Sissy join too?" Ana had asked.

"I think Sissy will have to sit in the stands with us and cheer you on." Mama had laughed. "Right, Aaron?"

Ana and Andrew's new baby brother, Aaron, burped, and everyone had laughed.

Now that basketball season was over, it was Andrew's turn to pick a sport.

"I want to join the baseball team," Andrew told his family over dinner one night. "Will you help me prepare for tryouts, Papa?" he asked.

"Of course," Papa said. "This weekend, we can go to the park and practice."

"Me and Sissy are coming too!" Ana said excitedly.

"Alright!" Andrew did a wiggle dance. He couldn't wait.

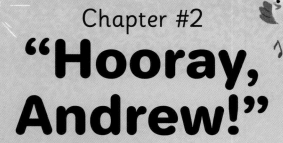

Chapter #2
"Hooray, Andrew!"

The sun was shining brightly. Birds were singing. It was the perfect afternoon to play baseball.

At the park, Andrew and Papa practiced throwing and catching. Ana watched as they threw the baseball back and forth. Every time Andrew caught the ball in his glove, she cheered.

"Way to go, Andrew!" Ana and Sissy clapped.

"OK, Andrew. Now it's time to practice hitting the ball with your bat," Papa said.

Andrew thought hitting the baseball with his bat would be easy. But it wasn't. Sometimes, he hit the baseball. And sometimes, he swung his bat and missed.

"Keep trying!" Ana encouraged.

Andrew and Papa practiced every evening until it was time for tryouts.

"Good luck, Andrew!" Mama, Papa, and Ana hugged Andrew the day he tried out for the team. After tryouts, the coach would send his parents an email to let them know whether Andrew made the team.

That evening, Papa's computer made a "ding" sound. "I think I just received the email we've been waiting for."

from: Baseball Team Coach
CONGRATULATIONS

"Well, did I make the team?" Andrew asked.

"Yes, you did!" Papa read the email and smiled.

"Congratulations!" Mama said.

"Hooray, Andrew!" Ana and Sissy cheered.

Even baby Aaron giggled.

Andrew couldn't wait to attend his first practice.

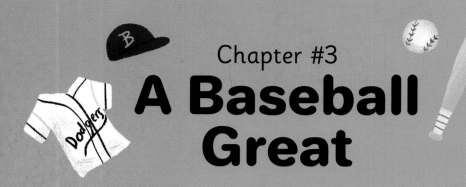

Chapter #3
A Baseball Great

Andrew had fun practicing with his teammates. But the night before their first big game, Andrew was nervous. He had never played baseball in front of a large crowd.

"There's going to be a lot of strangers at the game tomorrow," Andrew said with concern.

"Don't worry," Ana encouraged. "We'll be there to support you. And your friends will too."

"That's right," Mama agreed.

"At the big game tomorrow, I want you to think of Jackie Robinson," Papa said.

"Who is he?" Ana asked.

"Can I tell her?" Andrew's baseball coach had told the team about Jackie Robinson.

Papa smiled. "We can all tell her."

"Jackie Robinson was a famous African American baseball player," Andrew began. "He was one of the first African Americans to play Major League Baseball."

"*Really*?" Ana exclaimed.

"That's right," Papa said. "So, I am pretty sure he was nervous with all the people watching his first big game."

"Jackie Robinson was also the first African American member of the Baseball Hall of Fame," Mama added.

"Jackie's the inspiration for our team's name." Andrew proudly pointed to his DC Dodgers uniform. "He played for the Brooklyn Dodgers."

Then Andrew made a determined face. "Jackie Robinson is one of the greatest baseball players ever, and tomorrow, I'm going to be brave, just like he was!"

The next day, when Andrew stepped up to bat, he thought of Jackie Robinson. The pitcher threw the ball, but Andrew swung and missed.

"Strike one!" the umpire shouted.

Andrew swung and missed the second pitch too.

"Strike two!"

"C'mon, Andrew!" Ana cheered.
"Think of Jackie Robinson!"

The pitcher threw the baseball.
Andrew swung his bat and hit the
ball. It went flying through the air.

"Yay!" Everyone cheered as Andrew ran until he touched home plate.

"A home run!"

Chapter #4
Take Me Out to the . . .

Andrew's family and friends were so proud of him. His teammates patted him on the back and said, "Good job!"

After the game, Andrew and his teammates went to celebrate their first big game. Papa drove them to the pizza parlor. After they ate, Papa took a picture of Andrew standing with his coach and teammates.

When Papa and Andrew got home,
Mama and Ana yelled, "Surprise!"

There were balloons. And Mama
and Ana had baked chocolate
cupcakes—Andrew's favorite. Aaron
was even wearing a T-shirt that said
"Proud Little Brother."

"Oh boy!" Andrew did a wiggle dance, and everyone laughed.

"I have a surprise for you too." Papa smiled as he handed Andrew an envelope. "Well, it's a surprise for all of us actually."

"Hurry up and open it!" Ana squealed.

"OK, OK!" Andrew laughed. Carefully, he opened the envelope and pulled out five tickets.

"Where are we going?" Ana asked. "Me and Sissy can't wait to find out!"

"Family Night at Nationals Park."
Andrew read the wording on the
ticket passes. "We're going to watch a
professional ball game. In a stadium
just like one Jackie Robinson used to
play in!"

"Wow!" Ana hugged Sissy. "This is going to be so much fun!"

"Oh yeah, oh yeah!" Then, Andrew did a wiggle dance as he sang, "Take me out to the ball game!"